SOME FROM THE MOON

Farrar, Straus and Giroux • New York

SOME FROM THE SUN

Poems and Songs for Everyone

MARGOT ZEMACH

Pages 39–44 were designed by Kaethe Zemach-Bersin, using a portion of Margot Zemach's unfinished autobiography, previously unpublished artwork, and photographs from the Zemach family archives.

The photograph of Margot Zemach on page 39 was taken by Dan Robbin and is used with his permission.

Art on page 44 is used with the permission of Mertis L. Shekeloff.

Distributed in Canada by Douglas & McIntyre Ltd.

Color separations by Chroma Graphics PTE Ltd.

Printed and bound in the United States of America by Berryville Graphics

Typography by Filomena Tuosto

First edition, 2001

1 3 5 7 9 10 8 6 4 2

Library of Congress Cataloging-in-Publication Data

Zemach, Margot.

Some from the moon, some from the sun : poems and songs for everyone / Margot Zemach.— 1st ed.

p.   cm.

Summary: An illustrated collection of traditional poems and songs, including "This Little Pig Went to Market," "Brave News is Come to Town," and "Bingo."

ISBN 0-374-39960-3

1. Nursery rhymes. 2. Children's poetry. 3. Children's songs—Texts. [1. Nursery rhymes. 2. Songs.] I. Title.

PZ8.3.Z385 So 2001

398.8—dc21

00-67695

For Ariella, Gabriel, Giordan, Hannah, Julian, Laeka, Talya, and Twyla

Baby and I
   Were baked in a pie,
The gravy was wonderful hot.
   We had nothing to pay
   To the baker that day
And so we crept out of the pot.

Fishes swim in water clear,
Birds fly up into the air,
Serpents creep along the ground,
Boys and girls run round and round.

Pussy cat sits beside the fire,
    So pretty and so fair.
In walks the little dog,
    Ah, Miss Pussy, are you there?
How do you do, Miss Pussy?
    Miss Pussy, how do you do?
I thank you kindly, Mr. Dog,
    I'm very well, and you?

I gave a little party,
This afternoon at three,
It was very small,
Three guests in all,
Just I, myself, and me.
Myself ate up the sandwiches,
While I drank up the tea,
And it was I who ate the pie
And passed the cake to me.

Chook, chook, chook, chook, chook,

Good morning, Mrs. Hen.

How many chickens have you got?

Madam, I've got ten.

Four of them are yellow,

And four of them are brown,

And two of them are speckled red,

The nicest in the town.

Six little mice sat down to spin;
Pussy passed by and she peeped in.
What are you doing, my little men?
Weaving coats for gentlemen.
Shall I come in and cut off your threads?
No, no, Mistress Pussy, you'd bite off our heads.
Oh, no, I'll not; I'll help you to spin.
That may be so, but you don't come in.

Here we go around, around,
And here we go around,
Here we go around, around,
Till our skirts drag on the ground.

When Jacky's a good boy,
  He shall have cakes and custard;
But when he does nothing but cry,
  He shall have nothing but mustard.

Here am I,
Little Jumping Joan;
When nobody's with me
I'm all alone.

The elephants are coming
One by one,
Some from the moon,
Some from the sun.

I'm the king of the castle,
Get down, you dirty rascal!

There she goes,
There she goes,
All dressed up in her Sunday clothes.

There was a farmer had a dog,
His name was little Bingo,
B·I·N·G·O, B·I·N·G·O, B·I·N·G·O,
And his name was little Bingo!

This little pig went to market,
This little pig stayed home,
This little pig had roast beef,
This little pig had none,
And this little pig cried,
Wee wee wee,
all the way home.

There was a lady loved a swine,
Honey dear, said she,
Will you be my own true love?
Oink, oink, dear, said he.

Warm hands, warm,
The men have gone to plow,
If you want to warm your hands,
Warm your hands now.

Brush hair, brush,
The men have gone to plow,
If you want to brush your hair,
Brush your hair now.

Nobody loves me,
Everybody hates me,
I'm going out to eat worms,
Long, skinny, slimy ones,
Big, fat, juicy ones,
Itsy bitsy teeny ones.
See how they wiggle and squirm!
Yum! Yum!

Birds they fly and birds they rest,
Which pretty birdie do you like best?

The grapes hang green upon the vine,
I choose you as a friend of mine,
I choose you out of all the rest,
The reason is I love you best.

1, 2, 3, 4,

Mary at the cottage door,

5, 6, 7, 8,

Eating cherries off a plate.

He loves me,
  He don't,
He'll have me,
  He won't,
He would if he could,
But he can't,
  So he don't.

Sleep, baby, sleep,
Thy father guards the sheep;
Thy mother shakes the dreamland tree
And from it fall sweet dreams for thee,
Sleep, baby, sleep.

Sleep, baby, sleep,
Our cottage vale is deep;
The little lamb is on the green,
With woolly fleece so soft and clean,
Sleep, baby, sleep.

Hannah Bantry,

In the pantry,

Gnawing at a mutton bone;

How she gnawed it,

How she clawed it,

When she found herself alone.

Brave news is come to town,
Brave news is carried;
Brave news is come to town,
Jemmy Dawson's married.

First he got a porridge pot,
Then he bought a ladle;
Then he got a wife and child,
And then he bought a cradle.

When a big tree falls and people aren't near,
Does it really make a noise if no one can hear?

Sleep, my child, and peace attend thee,
All through the night,
Guardian angels God will send thee,
All through the night.

Star light, star bright,
First star I see tonight,
Wish I may, wish I might,
Have the wish I wish tonight.

Margot Zemach

"If there are only cornflakes and mustard in the kitchen,
it's a great thing to be able to paint chocolate pudding."

Margot Zemach and Poppa Dog

ABOUT HER LIFE AND WORK, Margot Zemach wrote:

I was born in November 1931. Like many people then, my family was out of work, hungry, and on the move. I remember watching the telephone wires looping on and on against the sky as we traveled across the country.

Watercolor ink, 1978

For a while I stayed in Oklahoma with my grandparents. There I was happiest playing in the backyard with a hose, a pail of water, and the mud.

Watercolor ink, 1978

Age 3

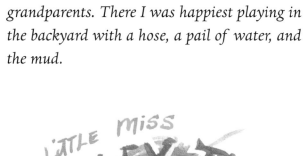

Though I admired Shirley Temple with all her curls and ruffles, and dreamed of going to Hollywood to play with her in her real-as-life playhouse, I felt uneasy. After all, how would I get there?

Watercolor ink, 1978

Crayon and ink, 1939

Later, living with my parents in New York and then Los Angeles, drawing became a good way to keep myself company. I would draw the same pretty girl over and over again, or I would draw entire villages ranging over a whole page, with a schoolhouse here and a drugstore there, and trees full of fruit. But usually I drew elves and fairies or people dancing.

Age 8

Poster paint, 1939

I never ever had enough paper. I drew on any scrap of paper I could find: napkins, the backs of envelopes, even tissues. If I was lucky, I had a box of crayons or a set of paints from the ten-cent store.

Poster paint and pencil, 1942

I drew after school and in most of my free time. I liked to sit in bed listening to radio dramas, illustrating stories or nursery rhymes for my own amusement: Cinderella, Rumpelstiltskin, Jack Be Nimble.

Poster paint and ink, 1947

Watercolor ink, 1978

Age 26

When I got older, I wanted to be an artist of social significance and went to art school to learn how to draw serious pictures.

Casein, 1956

But it became clear that I really enjoyed drawing and looking at funny pictures more than any other kind. So I thought about being either a great cartoonist or a children's book illustrator.

Pen and ink, 1959

Zemach

As it happened, my job in life has turned out to be illustrating books for children. I want to give life, movement, and humor to the words on paper. Making books, I can create my own theater and be in charge of everything: the actors, the sets, the costumes, and the way the stage is lit.

Children deserve detail, color, and excellence . . . the best an author and illustrator can do. The pictures have to be made "real." The food should be food you'd really want to eat and the bed should look so cozy that you'd want to climb in right away.

Studies for an unfinished work, watercolor ink, 1987

MARGOT ZEMACH illustrated over forty books, including thirteen with her husband and collaborator, Harve Zemach. During her distinguished career, she received many awards, including the Caldecott Medal in 1974 for *Duffy and the Devil*, written by Harve Zemach.

Watercolor ink, 1987

Margot and Harve working, while their daughters play—Denmark, 1970

Books Written and/or Illustrated by Margot Zemach

Small Boy Is Listening by Harve Zemach. Houghton Mifflin, 1959.

Take a Giant Step by Hannelore Hahn. Little, Brown, 1960.

A Hat with a Rose by Harve Zemach. Dutton, 1961.

Why Don't You Draw a Dog? by Marguerite Melcher. Little, Brown, 1962.

The Three Sillies: A Folktale. Holt, 1963.

The Last Dragon by Fleming Lee Blith. Lippincott, 1964.

Nail Soup: A Swedish Folktale, retold by Harve Zemach. Follett, 1964.

The Little, Tiny Woman. Bobbs-Merrill, 1965.

The Question Box by Jay Williams. Norton, 1965.

Salt: A Russian Tale, adapted from Alexander Afanasyev by Harve Zemach. Follett, 1965; Farrar, Straus and Giroux, 1977.

The Tricks of Master Dabble by Harve Zemach. Holt, 1965.

The Fisherman and His Wife by Jacob and Wilhelm Grimm. Norton, 1966.

The King of the Hermits and Other Stories by Jack Sendak. Farrar, Straus and Giroux, 1966.

Mommy, Buy Me a China Doll, adapted from an Ozark children's song by Harve Zemach. Follett, 1966; Farrar, Straus and Giroux, 1975.

The Speckled Hen: A Russian Nursery Rhyme, adapted by Harve Zemach. Holt, 1966.

Mazel and Shlimazel, or The Milk of a Lioness by Isaac Bashevis Singer. Farrar, Straus and Giroux, 1967.

Too Much Nose: An Italian Tale, adapted by Harve Zemach. Holt, 1967.

Harlequin by Rose Laura Mincieli. Knopf, 1968.

When Shlemiel Went to Warsaw and Other Stories by Isaac Bashevis Singer. Farrar, Straus and Giroux, 1968.

The Judge: An Untrue Tale by Harve Zemach. Farrar, Straus and Giroux, 1969.

Awake and Dreaming by Harve Zemach. Farrar, Straus and Giroux, 1970.

Alone in the Wild Forest by Isaac Bashevis Singer. Farrar, Straus and Giroux, 1971.

Favorite Fairy Tales Told in Denmark by Virginia Haviland. Little, Brown, 1971.

A Penny a Look: An Old Story, retold by Harve Zemach. Farrar, Straus and Giroux, 1971.

Simon Boom Gives a Wedding by Yuri Suhl. Four Winds, 1972.

Duffy and the Devil: A Cornish Tale, retold by Harve Zemach. Farrar, Straus and Giroux, 1973.

The Foundling and Other Tales of Prydain by Lloyd Alexander. Holt, 1973.

The Princess and Froggie by Harve and Kaethe Zemach. Farrar, Straus and Giroux, 1975.

Hush, Little Baby. Dutton, 1976.

It Could Always Be Worse: A Yiddish Folktale. Farrar, Straus and Giroux, 1976.

Naftali the Storyteller and His Horse, Sus, and Other Stories by Isaac Bashevis Singer. Farrar, Straus and Giroux, 1976.

The Frogs Who Wanted a King and Other Songs from La Fontaine, collected by Edward Smith. Four Winds, 1977.

To Hilda for Helping. Farrar, Straus and Giroux, 1977.

Self-portrait: Margot Zemach. Addison-Wesley, 1978.

The Fisherman and His Wife by Jacob and Wilhelm Grimm; translated by Randall Jarrell. Farrar, Straus and Giroux, 1980.

The Cat's Elbow and Other Secret Languages, collected by Alvin Schwartz. Farrar, Straus and Giroux, 1982.

Come On, Patsy by Zilpha Keatley Snyder. Atheneum, 1982.

Jake and Honeybunch Go to Heaven. Farrar, Straus and Giroux, 1982.

The Little Red Hen: An Old Story. Farrar, Straus and Giroux, 1983.

Molly, McCullough, & Tom the Rogue by Kathleen Stevens. Crowell, 1983.

The Sign in Mendel's Window by Mildred Phillips. Macmillan, 1985.

The Three Wishes: An Old Story. Farrar, Straus and Giroux, 1986.

Two Foolish Cats by Yoshiko Uchida. McElderry Books, 1987.

The Chinese Mirror, adapted from a Korean folktale by Mirra Ginsburg. Harcourt, 1988.

The Enchanted Umbrella by Odette Meyers. Harcourt, 1988.

Sing a Song of Popcorn: Every Child's Book of Poems, selected by Beatrice Schenk de Regniers and illustrated by nine Caldecott Medalists. Scholastic, 1988.

The Three Little Pigs: An Old Story. Farrar, Straus and Giroux, 1988.

All God's Critters Got a Place in the Choir by Bill Staines. Dutton, 1989.

Receiving news about winning the Caldecott Medal